fun AT BURRA CREEK

STORY AND PICTURES
BY EMMA LAUREN

*For my darling boy, Max, who loves the Burra Creek
and with thanks to my family and friends
for their support.*

Published by Emma Lauren

ISBN: 978-0-6452984-0-6 (paperback)

First edition, 2021

For book orders and enquiries, contact:
emmalauren.childrensbooks@gmail.com

A catalogue record for this book is available from the National Library of Australia

Acknowledgement of Country, courtesy of Burra Early Learning Centre:

Thank you to the Ngadjuri people for the plants, the animals, the stories and for letting us play.

We promise to look after the land of the Ngadjuri every day.

Do you know the Burra Creek?

It has countless stories to share.

This one's about a boy named **Max**...

and his yellow duckie, **Claire.**

These two pals just LOVED the creek
with its very many thrills.
It all began on one fine day
with Max's persuasive skills...

When splashing in his bubble bath
and chatting with his mum
about their outing to the creek,
he pleaded...

"Sure, why not?!" his mummy said —
after all, it could be fun...

to see these pals outside together
playing in the sun.

So they packed a bag and grabbed the trike
and loaded up the boot
and headed to the Burra Creek
for what was bound to be a hoot!

"We're here!!"
Max yelled, triumphantly,
as he hurried out the car...

He fetched his trike and cluey Claire
jumped on the handlebar!

They whizzed across the baby bridge
that rests above the brook
and headed to the duckie zone —
Claire was keen to get a look.

She wondered, *Will they like me?*
Those creek ducks, big and tall.
My quack is soft and squeaky
and I'm only very small.

These thoughts filled Claire with worry —
her excitement turned to fear.
Before, she'd wanted to meet them.
Now she longed to disappear!

"Max, I'm scared,"
she squeaked with fright,
not knowing what to do.

"It's okay, Claire — it's new for you.
When I first met the duckies,
I was a bit scared too!"

"Yes, *good* thought!" Claire decided,
now feeling more upbeat.
"Come on, let's go," she chirped.
"I've got some new friends to meet!"

They had a special bag in tow
for their friendly feathered chums.
The ducks soon waddled up the bank
to fill up hungry tums!

Meeting – and treating! – the ducks was GREAT.
Claire was proud she gave it a go
and thankful to her best friend, Max,
whose kindness helped her grow.

Once the duckies' tums were fed,
it was time to 'Nature Boat' —
a little game Max liked to play
where you send a leaf afloat.

You drop it from the little bridge
on the upstream side
and if the water flow is right,
it works like a waterslide!

Max and Claire, they found a leaf
that had fallen to the ground.
They launched it from atop the bridge
— it didn't make a sound.

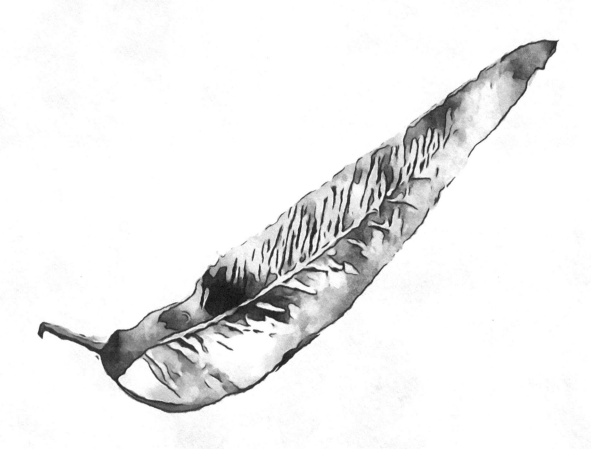

They quickly ran across the bridge
to the downstream side
and waited for their nature boat —
would it last the ride?

Above that stream sat two pairs
of waiting, watchful eyes —
cheering on their nature boat
when suddenly...

SURPRISE!

There it was, that little leaf
— its maiden voyage a success!
Max and Claire were very happy
with their boat — it did impress!

Next, Max wanted to dip his feet
in that trickling stream.
His shoes were off, and Claire was in –
it was a rubber duckie's dream!

MAX AND CLAIRE
2nd may

They played and splashed and posed
for happy snaps for Max's mum.
"Lunchtime now!" she smiled at them,
knowing they wouldn't want to come.

She grabbed two towels to tempt them out
— one rectangle and one square.
The bigger one was for Max
and the little was for Claire!

They ate their lunch and dried their bods
at a table in the sun
and after lunch was gobbled up
a new adventure was begun.

They ran across the nearby lawn
to the playground gate —
busting now to get inside
and play on all that did await!

The swings and slides and kangaroo
were all about to meet
Max's special buddy, Claire,
for the first time — what a treat!

They climbed, and slid
and swung their bodies high into the sky...

Max's mummy promised
she would bring them back again
and so they rode back to the car,
the two pals thinking, *When?!*

and bounced around on Horsey's back
until it was time to say goodbye...

"Not forever, just for now,"
Max's mummy said.
"The day is getting late you know...
it will soon be time for bed!"

Max dropped his lip and cuddled Claire
— he didn't want to go.
He loved this place so very much
that leaving was a blow!

Oh, what fun this pair had had
doing all the little things
that warm the heart and soothe the soul
and give the mind its wings.

You, too, can have a blast
down at the Burra Creek.
Just pack your bag and sense of fun
and come and take a peek!

Lightning Source UK Ltd.
Milton Keynes UK
UKHW050631111121
393768UK00003B/115